Deep gratitude to Father Jacques de Foiard Brown, whose hand-drawn maps
and stories of solitary retreats on islands in St. Brandon's Atoll in the
Indian Ocean guided my imaginings of Snook's adventures on Avocaire.

M. N.

*"Faith is . . . like loving someone who is out there in the darkness but
never appears, no matter how loudly you call."* — Ingmar Bergman

For Jen, Finn, and Sawyer.
No storm will separate us!

T. B. E.

Text copyright © 2010 by Marilyn Nelson
Illustrations copyright © 2010 by Timothy Basil Ering

First paperback edition 2012

The Library of Congress has cataloged the hardcover edition as follows:

Nelson, Marilyn, date.
Snook alone / Marilyn Nelson ; illustrated by Timothy Basil Ering. — 1st ed.
p. cm.
Summary: Through the power of faith, a monk named Abba Jacob and his loyal rat terrier,
Snook, are reunited after being separated by a ferocious storm.
ISBN 978-0-7636-2667-9 (hardcover)
[1. Dogs — Fiction. 2. Monks — Fiction. 3. Friendship — Fiction.
4. Faith — Fiction.] I. Ering, Timothy B., ill. II. Title.
PZ7.N43557Sn 2010
[E] — dc22   2009049040

ISBN 978-0-7636-6120-5 (paperback)

12 13 14 15 16 17 CCP 10 9 8 7 6 5 4 3 2 1
Printed in Shenzhen, Guangdong, China

This book was typeset in Archetype.
The illustrations were done in acrylic and ink.

Candlewick Press
99 Dover Street
Somerville, Massachusetts 02144

visit us at www.candlewick.com

THIS CANDLEWICK BOOK BELONGS TO:

_____

_____

_____

Snook Alone

Marilyn Nelson

illustrated by

Timothy Basil Ering

CANDLEWICK PRESS

bba Jacob was a monk who lived in a hermitage on an

island in a faraway sea.

His job was to pray and work, pray and work, pray and work all day.

Abba Jacob's little rat terrier, Snook,

was a black-on-white bundle of intelligent energy

with brown cheeks and eyebrows and black floppy ears.

His job was to catch the mice and rats

that scurried through Abba Jacob's kitchen at night,

and by day to be Abba Jacob's shadow.

When Abba Jacob got up before dawn,
Snook stretched his back legs and yawned,
then he trotted at his friend's heels up the steps
into the chapel. Abba Jacob closed the door,
sat down on a stool, put his feet flat on the floor,
straightened his back, took a long, deep breath,
and closed his eyes.
Snook scratched behind both ears,
curled up on the straw mat,
sighed, and closed his.
He heard
the wind in the sugar canes, the me-singing birds,
a distant, insistent rooster, a rumble of trucks,
and the bee-buzzing of motorbikes.
He heard the chatter and laughter of women
on their way to work in the cane fields.
When his friend stood up and bowed
toward the little table in the corner
where there were seashells and a candle
and a picture of a lady holding a child,
Snook shook himself and followed his friend out
into the soft dawn light. They stepped down
  the stairs
and went to work.

Sometimes they worked in the sugar cane.
Snook prowled the forest of stalks, and rats
squealed with terror at his approach.
Sometimes Snook routed a sleeping hare
and won a high-speed race
with a delicious prize.

Sometimes they watered the coconut palms.
(Abba Jacob used a green hose.)
Sometimes Snook watched his friend harvest
papayas or mangoes, guavas or breadfruit.
Sometimes Snook lay, alertly waiting,
and watched Abba Jacob work
on the plumbing or the wiring of the hermitage
or sweep out the guesthouse
or scrub the toilets.

Then they had breakfast. Abba Jacob gave Snook
the delicious, chewy rind of his slice of cheese
or flipped him the crust of his bread.
Sometimes Snook had a bite of fruit.
Then Abba Jacob swallowed a last slurp of tea
and put away his breakfast things.
Snook followed him to the fish pool
and prowled for mice while Abba Jacob
fed the carp and rescued
the toads, lizards, geckos, and the odd hedgehog
that had fallen in overnight.
Sometimes Abba Jacob washed his hands,
pulled a long white tunic over his shirt and trousers,
buckled on a worn brown leather belt,
got into his battered old car,
and drove away.

Snook waited.
He listened.
The wind, the birds,
human sounds from the road.
A frozen emptiness in time,
until one special car
rattling up the gravel drive
roused him to attention,
and he raced to meet it.

There was the occasional interruption
of humans stopping by, individually and as groups,
to talk with Abba Jacob.
But each day was a striped flag
of silence, work, food, silence, work, silence.

After the last silence,
Abba Jacob blew out the candle, bowed,
and walked down the steps and crossed the lawn
to his house to go to bed.
Snook slept on the veranda
on a green cushion,
with one ear periscoping out of sleep
and every sleeping muscle poised.

His friend rose to kneel again
when the night sang only of crickets,
and when the moon was high.
Snook followed him through the dark.
They climbed the stairs to the chapel
and descended into the silence.

Snook stood at the point of the bow, his black ears flapping.
The Society for the Preservation of St. Brandon's Atoll
had asked Abba Jacob to help them catalog
the plant and animal species on every island:
Île Cocos, Île Longue, Loup-Garou, Sirène, Puits à Eau, Albatross . . .
The catalogers were to make a quick circuit of the atoll
and return to home base. They were on a tight schedule:
one island a day for one week.
Snook was along to catch rats and mice,
whose overbred numbers were decimating
the sea-birds' nesting grounds.
The rats and mice ate eggs.
Snook was to eat them.
It was a good job.

Like the other islands, Avocaire
was a mile-long crescent of beach
surrounding a higher ground of pemphis marshes,
salt-resistant bushes, papaya and casuarina trees, and coconut palms,
with bare guano-covered circles where boobies, frigate birds,
   and terns nested.
What great micing!

Snook had never worked so hard.
A black line thickened on the horizon.
The mood of the sea darkened.
Ripples became waves;
waves became breakers.
Abba Jacob hurried toward the boat,
whistling and calling, "Snookie-boy! Come,
    Snook! Come!"

But there were still many unmarked
    casuarina trunks,
and rats that squealed with fear at
    Snook's approach.
Snook was very busy.

"Snook! Snook!"
The wind snatched Abba Jacob's voice;
the waves muted his whistle.
"Snook! Snook!"
Then the boat rushed Abba Jacob to safety
with the other men in the expedition,
to ride out the gale
anchored in the lee of a larger island.

Casuarina branches thirty feet up
   roared like jet planes.
Palm fronds crashed; coconuts
   thumped to the ground and rolled.
Snook ran up and down the beach,
where the scent of Abba Jacob's
   footprints
disappeared into noisy water. He
   barked into the wind.
His ears rode it like pennants; his legs
   braced against it.
But at last the wind bullied him into
   seeking shelter.
He spent the night in a cave of
   pemphis roots.
He slept fitfully,
his ears awash in noise.

In the morning
there were only faint sips of his friend's scent
left for Snook to drink in here and there.
He sat on the beach,
watching a band of clear sky fill with streaming light.

Snook was thirsty.
He sniffed past the squealing rats and mice
and the nesting birds' *queck-queck*
as they rose in alarm and formed a black spiral overhead.

He followed his nose to a sandy hollow
in a circle of velvet-leafed arguisia bushes.
There he dug, tentatively at first.
Then, as the scent of fresh water grew stronger,
he dug furiously, making the sand fly.
At last, he lapped sweet water.
Then he made his well larger,
and drank and drank.
On his way back down to the beach
he marked many trees.

In the morning there was no more trace
of Abba Jacob on Avocaire Island,
except inside Snook.
In the evening the sky unfurled a sea of stars
over the sea where Abba Jacob had disappeared.
Snook sat between two shiny-leaved scaevola shrubs,
which no dog on earth but he had ever marked,
and waited for his friend.

Snook woke up every morning before dawn.
He waited.
Then he foraged, moused, and drank.
Then he waited again.
The silence was black and empty.

The silence was lonely.
Snook sat on the beach.
Around him lay scattered bits
of pink and white coral, bright pieces of shells.

Snook listened to the silence,
to the wind and the waves.
He waited.

Snook's new home in the pemphis roots
was wind-sheltered, dry, and cozy.
He was curled there one night
as waves crashed and a crescent moon
rose naked over the reef and the lagoon.
Clack-clack! Clack-clack!
Something was scurrying closer.
Snook rushed out, barking a challenge.
A *Cardisoma* land crab,
as big as he was,
clacked its larger claw at him,
its stalk eyes expressionless as pebbles.
When Snook lunged, the crab
fended him off with its claw,
like a boxer with one giant glove.
Snook bravely defended his home,
but the crab forged ahead
like a robot tank.
It moved into Snook's warren,
claimed one corner,
and stayed. Snook curled
in the farthest corner
and watched all night.
In the silence, he listened.
The wind was his breathing.
The waves were his breath.

Snook foraged in tidal pools
and stalked the lagoon's warm shallows,
patiently waiting. When a slow fish
swam near, Snook pounced with a splash.
If he caught something,
he carried it to higher ground
and ate delicately.
If he caught nothing,
the waiting and the splash were pure play.
He learned to be cautious
of the prowling baby sharks,
with their taste for everything alive.
He learned to avoid
chasing mice into the guano beds
where the sea-birds nested.
What a cloud of foul dust that raised!

        Though he skirted them carefully,
        he had only to chase a mouse nearby
        to make the whole colony of boobies rise,
        in a shimmer of sound,
        and swoop, screeching and
        poking their beaks at his head.
        Over his shoulder as he ran away
        he saw the fluffy chicks
        sitting dumbfounded,
        like a field of white teddy bears.

Sometimes Snook watched the birds.
The fairy terns, arrowlike white creatures,
quick and agile, flew in mated pairs,
dive-bombing the sea and flying home
with little fishes dangling from their beaks
like handlebar mustaches.
The heavier, larger frigate birds
often robbed them of their catch
before they could get to their chicks.
The terns soared back for a new
catch, weaving together
like streaks of playful light,
every movement a synonym for joy.

Sometimes two fairy terns hovered
at Snook's eye level for seconds,
watching him with curious black eyes.

Snook faced the changing sea-light
spreading before him.
The wide pale beach
called up waves as far as he could see.
"My Snook."
He sat on his haunches
with his white front paws
neatly in front of him, side by side.
He sat with a straight little black-on-
　　white back.
He held his head up, his ears cocked.
He waited.
A frigate screamed.
The casuarinas shirred
or whistled
or roared.
The surf lapped the coral-strewn sand.
Wind was like breathing.
Snook watched the horizon
at dawn, noon, at sunset,
the incomprehensible vastness
was a closed door to his friend.
Breath was like waves.
Snook waited,
as he had waited for the Jubilation Day
rattle of his friend's car
on the driveway to their hermitage.
Every molecule listened for his friend.
Wind, breath, breath, waves.

A midnight commotion.
A disturbance of the island's peace.
Snook sprang to and sniffed for clues.
Something new was out there. . . .
He raced across sand dunes,
through clumps of arguisia.
In the coconut grove near the tip of
   the island,
he stood, quivering, his nose
   twitching, his ears alert.
By the shadow-casting light of a
   round moon,
he saw many large beings
lumbering slow and steady
out of the ocean
and up the beach.

Snook trembled.
They were very large.
Their bodies did not bend.
Some of them were using their wide
   back flippers
to scoop hollows in the sand.

Snook crept closer.
They seemed harmless, intent
on some mysterious, urgent business.
Snook walked gingerly among them,
his hackles raised.

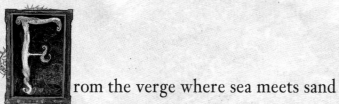rom the verge where sea meets sand
he heard splashing, thrashing,
live terror, a last rush,
a voracious hunger.
One of the beings, just emerging from inky
   water,
was something else's prey.
Something huge, something dreadful.
Snook growled.
With awkward flippers,
the prey scrabbled heavily up the beach.
The hunter hurled itself out of the sea
in burning bright pursuit.
Its dark striped body
was one sleek muscle
with rows of glittering teeth
and an omnivorous, fathomless eye.
It looked at Snook for one instant,
the way Snook looked at rats.
Then it snatched its prey by one flipper
and in one smooth arc muscled itself
and its flailing prey
back into its element.

By afternoon the northwest beach
had been scored by dozens of carapaces,
the high dry sand dug up and covered
by many graceless flippers.
But one last turtle was still digging.

Snook lay in the scant shade of a suriana
and watched her labor.
Her beak open as if to pant,
she dug with one rear flipper
and one healed stump.
Her eyes, half closed,
streamed tears.
She seemed as old as the world.

She laid dozens of eggs,
covered them with sand,
and as dark fell dragged her weight
back to the deep.

Snook lifted his nose
and howled.
In the sky, Orion
released an arrow:
Pffft!

For days after, the sea
was a green turtle's weeping eye.
Snook waited for his friend's soothing voice
to emerge from its hiding place beneath the waves,
from its hiding place beneath the wind in the trees.
Snook sat still enough
to find the shared silence
of Abba Jacob's chapel
under the rhythmic surge of surf.
He could almost hear,
almost make out,
like a whisper in a cyclone,
the voice he was waiting to hear.
"Good boy, Snook. Good dog."

Snook wagged his tail.

There were finds of flotsam:
full moons of fishing buoys,
tidbits of sharks' meals,
a plastic soft-drink bottle,
some pieces of Styrofoam.

Some of this was good to eat.
Some of it was good to play with.
Some was good to roll in.
Thus camouflaged,
Snook stalked his island
in a wolf-size cloud of stink.
The rats didn't know what hit them.

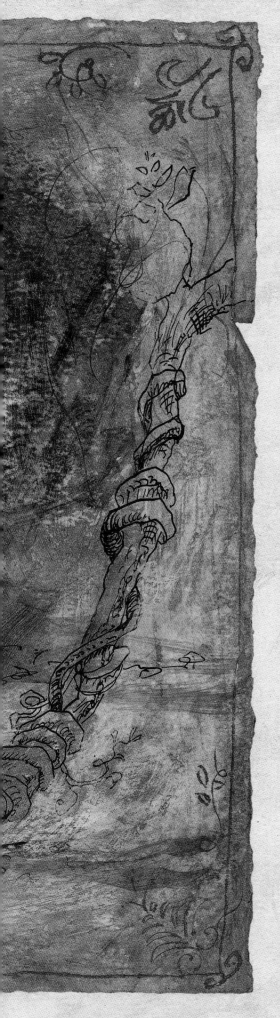

But Avocaire Island was the center
of a vast circle of longing.
And from one unknown direction
Snook's longing came back to him,
mirrored in a fractal of moving sea-light,
one flicker of which
was Abba Jacob's prayer.

Wind, breathing.
Breath, waves.

"Good dog."
Love went in Snook now
from one end of Avocaire to the other,
from east to west, south to north.
Whether the noon sun blazed overhead
or the Southern Cross blinked down at night,
whether he was working or eating or dozing,
Snook was always waiting now
in his friend's silence.
Abba Jacob's silence was the wind.
It was the sea.
It was the love in Snook,
compassionate and wise as the turtle's eye.

One day the good ending came.
A dot grew to be a fishing craft,
which sent an inflatable motorboat
with a tall man standing in its prow.
Snook trembled on the beach, watching.

Then he jumped and raced in a yapping circle
of pee-dribbling delight.
As the boat skimmed sand
and the man at the tiller cut the motor,

Abba Jacob splashed out.
He ran to meet the barking somersault
that leaped into his arms.
"Oh, Snook," he said. "Good dog!"
Snook whimpered against his friend's chest.
He licked his chin, his ears. Abba Jacob laughed.
"You silly, 'orrible little beastie, you.

"Good dog, Snookie-boy.
Good dog!"

Marilyn Nelson is the author of many acclaimed books for young people and adults, including *Carver: A Life in Poems*, a Newbery Honor Book and Coretta Scott King Honor Book, and *A Wreath for Emmett Till*, a Michael L. Printz Honor Book and Coretta Scott King Honor Book. She is also the translator of *The Ladder* and the co-translator of *A Little Bitty Man and Other Poems for the Very Young*, both by Halfdan Rasmussen. She lives in East Haddam, Connecticut.

Timothy Basil Ering is the illustrator of the Newbery Medal–winning *The Tale of Despereaux* by Kate DiCamillo and *Finn Throws a Fit!* by David Elliott. He is also the author-illustrator of *The Story of Frog Belly Rat Bone* and *Necks Out for Adventure!* He lives in Massachusetts.